This book belongs to:

_____

Special thanks to Susan and Diane.

Published 2021 by Flowered Press
Copyright© 2021 by Hayley Rose

Text and design by Hayley Rose
Illustrations by Bright Jungle Studios

ISBN: 978-1-950842-21-6

Library of Congress Control Number: 2020925952

Flowered Press
8776 E.Shea Blvd., #106-213
Scottsdale, AZ 85260

www.HayleyRose.com

Gomer
the
Gassy Goat

A Fart-Filled Tale

Written by Hayley Rose

Illustrated by Bright Jungle Studios

Gomer the goat has a problem.
He farts A LOT!

TOOT TOOT

He's a GASSY goat.

Gomer the goat has a problem.
He farts A LOT!

TOOT TOOT

AND, he LIKES it!

He's a SASSY, gassy goat.

Gomer the goat has a problem.
He farts A LOT!

TOOT TOOT

He LIKES it.
AND, he makes FUNNY faces when he farts.

He's a SILLY, sassy, gassy goat.

Gomer the goat has a problem.
He farts A LOT!

TOOT TOOT

He LIKES it.
He makes FUNNY faces.
BUT, he always APOLOGIZES.

He's a CLASSY, silly, sassy, gassy goat.

Gomer the goat has a problem.
He farts A LOT!

TOOT TOOT

He LIKES it.
He makes FUNNY faces.
He APOLOGIZES.
AND, his farts STINK!

Gomer the goat has a problem.
He farts A LOT!

TOOT TOOT

He LIKES it.
He makes FUNNY faces.
He APOLOGIZES.
His farts STINK.
AND, he's HAPPY about it!

He's a SMILEY, smelly, classy, silly, sassy, gassy goat.

Gomer the goat has a problem.
He farts A LOT!

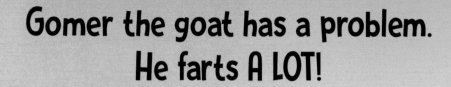

TOOT TOOT

He LIKES it.
He makes FUNNY faces.
He APOLOGIZES.
His farts STINK.
He's HAPPY about it.
AND, his farts are really LOUD!

He's a NOISY, smiley, smelly, classy, silly, sassy, gassy goat.

Gomer the goat has a problem.
He farts A LOT!

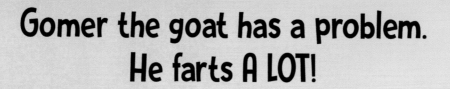

He LIKES it.
He makes FUNNY faces.
He APOLOGIZES.
His farts STINK.
He's HAPPY about it.
His farts are LOUD.
AND, he wants to know if YOU fart!

Gomer the goat has a problem.
He farts A LOT!

TOOT TOOT

He LIKES it.
He makes FUNNY faces.
He APOLOGIZES.
His farts STINK.
He's HAPPY about it.
His farts are LOUD.
He wants to know if YOU fart.
AND, he even farts during GOAT YOGA!

He's a TRENDY-BENDY, nosy, noisy, smiley, smelly, classy, silly, sassy, gassy goat.

Gomer the goat has a problem.
He farts A LOT!

TOOT TOOT

He LIKES it.
He makes FUNNY faces.
He APOLOGIZES.
His farts STINK.
He's HAPPY about it.
His farts are LOUD.
He wants to know if YOU fart.
He farts during GOAT YOGA.
AND, farts make him LAUGH!

He's a GIGGLY, trendy-bendy, nosy, noisy, smiley, smelly, classy, silly, sassy, gassy goat.

Gomer the goat has a problem.
He farts A LOT!

TOOT TOOT

He LIKES it.
He makes FUNNY faces.
He APOLOGIZES.
His farts STINK.
He's HAPPY about it.
His farts are LOUD.
He wants to know if YOU fart.
He farts during GOAT YOGA.
His farts make him LAUGH.
AND, he's very POPULAR!

He's a FRIENDLY, giggly, trendy-bendy, nosy, noisy, smiley, smelly, classy, silly, sassy, gassy goat.

Gomer the goat has a problem.
He farts A LOT!

TOOT TOOT

He LIKES it.
He makes FUNNY faces.
He APOLOGIZES.
His farts STINK.
He's HAPPY about it.
His farts are LOUD.
He wants to know if YOU fart.
He farts during GOAT YOGA.
His farts make him LAUGH.
He's very POPULAR.
AND, he farts in his PAJAMAS!

He's a SLEEPY, friendly, giggly, trendy-bendy, nosy, noisy, smiley, smelly, classy, silly, sassy, gassy goat.

Goodnight.